My Music Box
Little classical masterpieces for my baby

Whatever a composer's reputation, what really matters is the moods they create and our love for their compositions. While Tchaikovsky flows into Lyadov, and Debussy and Ibert make a fine pairing, this collection of miniature masterpieces for two- or four-hand piano doesn't tell a story. Rather, it takes us back to an earlier time—the time of Russian and French aristocracies in the late nineteenth and early twentieth centuries.

As you enter the intimate, dreamlike world of each composer, you will rediscover the joys and fears of childhood, with its strong yet fleeting emotions, enhanced by the powerful colours of your imagination!

1 In a Boat
Claude Debussy (1862–1918)

In a Boat (En bateau) is the first of four movements comprising the *Short Suite (Petite Suite)*, composed by Claude Debussy for four-hand piano between 1886 and 1889.

A shiny boat sails proudly
on the large pool at the Tuileries…
In this garden filled with the scents of spring,
it is 1900. Look—a young, bright-eyed sailor!

2 Children's Quarrels after Games
Modest Mussorgsky (1839–1881)

Children's Quarrels after Games (Tuileries, Disputes d'enfants après jeux) is a movement in B major from *Pictures at an Exhibition*, a series of piano pieces composed by Modest Mussorgksky in 1874.

"Wahhhhh, Wahhhhh!
Mama, he started it!"
Children quarrelling, prattling sounds, and mischief
all depicted through Mussorgsky's music.

3 Dance of the Sugar Plum Fairy

Pyotr Ilyich Tchaikovsky (1840–1893)

Taken from *The Nutcracker* ballet, *Dance of the Sugar Plum Fairy* is one of the most famous classical pieces, thanks, in part, to the use of a revolutionary new instrument: the celesta. In this transcription for four-hand piano, the musicians imitate the instrument's crystal-clear sonorities.

Once upon a time, a Sugar Plum Fairy lived in a castle.
With a wave of her magic wand,
she could fulfill your sweetest dreams
by transforming any object into candy, fruit jellies,
licorice, or some other sweet delight.

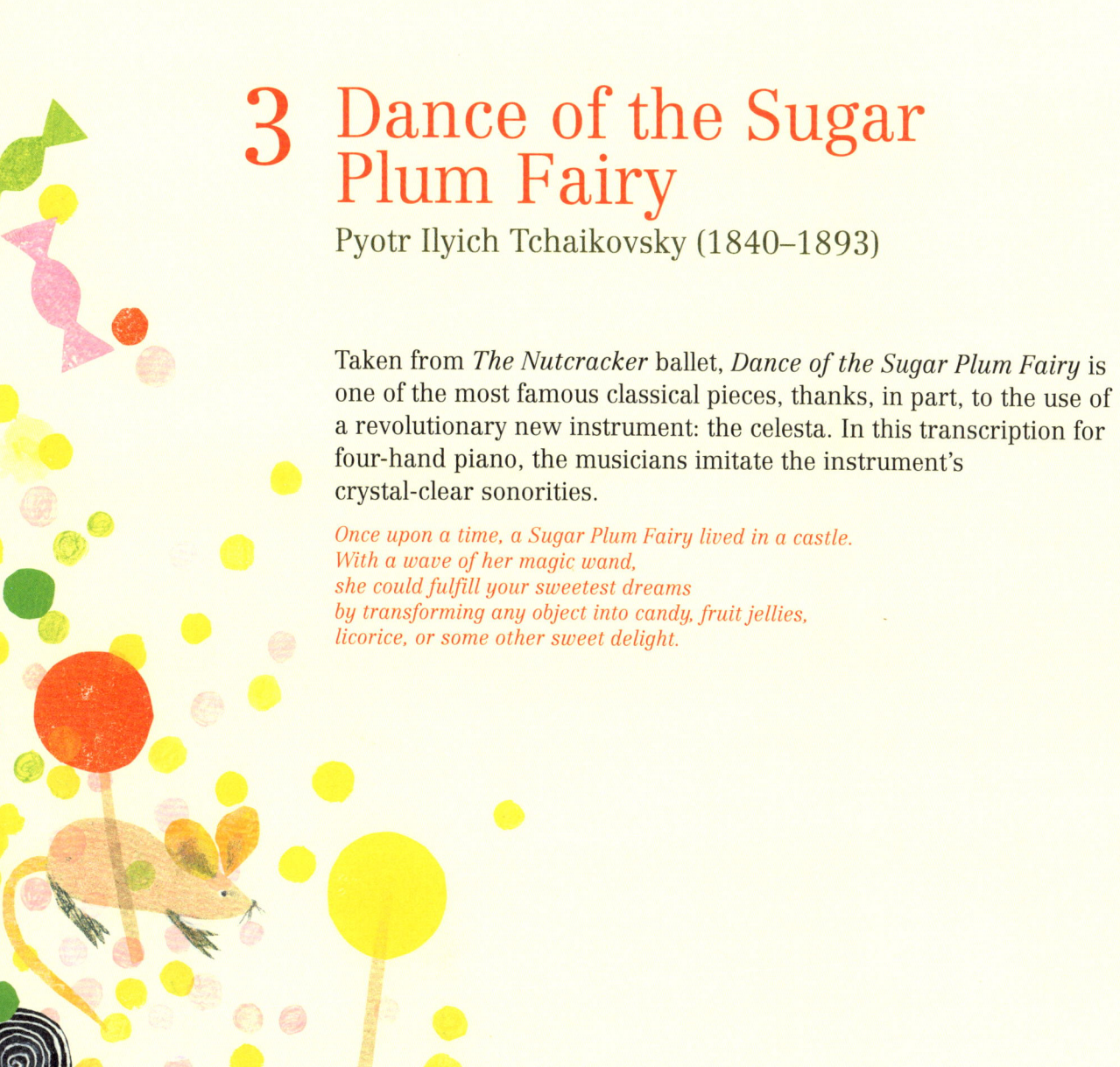

4 Serenade for the Doll
Claude Debussy (1862–1918)

Serenade for the Doll (Sérénade à la poupée) is the third piece in Claude Debussy's famous suite, *The Children's Corner*, a collection of six piano pieces dedicated to his daughter Claude-Emma, affectionately known as Chouchou. He also dedicated his popular ballet, *The Toy-Box (La Boîte à joujoux),* to her.

t was a doll with long legs and big, open eyes.
Neither girl nor boy, the doll dreamt of strange, fantastic landscapes,
mountains and plains, sunrises, and starry nights.
This serenade is an invitation to travel.

5 Trumpet and Drum
Georges Bizet (1838–1875)

In 1871, the renowned composer of the opera *Carmen*, Georges Bizet, wrote *Children's Games (Jeux d'enfants)*, Opus 22, a cycle of twelve miniature pieces for four-hand piano. *Trumpet and Drum (Trompette et tambour)* is the sixth piece in the collection, his final work for the piano.

In a bedroom full of toys,
a small boy wears a cocked hat and looks over his armies:
"Wooden soldiers, lead soldiers and
Paper mâché soldiers, salute your general!"

6 Fairy Tale, Opus 26, No. 1, in E-flat major

Nikolai Medtner (1880–1951)

Prior to the Russian Revolution, Nikolai Medtner was a pianist and composer with a reputation on par with friends and colleagues Sergei Rachmaninoff and Alexander Scriabin. With a hundred piano pieces and as many songs to his credit, Medtner is famous for his many fairy tales for piano, which express Russian folklore in music even more than the works of his celebrated contemporaries.

Over the shimmering sand,
the sun slowly sets as birds fly away.
It seems as though nothing bad
could ever happen.

7 Golliwogg's Cake-walk
Claude Debussy (1862–1918)

This dynamic and iconoclastic piece is by far the best-known movement from *The Children's Corner*. In this composition, Claude Debussy draws inspiration from ragtime and jazz, and of course, the cake-walk, a dance originally performed by enslaved African Americans on plantations. Today, the golliwog and cake-walk should be contextualized as expressions of racism present in the late nineteenth and early twentieth century.

Here is a doll unlike any other:
All she cares about is bothering the other dolls!
The other toys are all targets of her ceaseless
jokes and taunting.
A bit like Debussy himself, by the way!

8 Prelude, Opus 10, No. 1, in D-flat major

Anatoly Lyadov (1855–1914)

Born into a large family of Russian artists, Anatoly Lyadov composed some hundred orchestral, vocal, and instrumental works. A student of Nikolai Rimsky-Korsakov and later a teacher of Sergei Prokofiev, he would have been the composer of *The Firebird*, but for his legendary laziness, which led Ballets Russes director Sergei Diaghilev to replace him with a complete unknown: Igor Stravinsky. As this prelude demonstrates, his music for piano often takes the form of exquisite miniatures.

Listen… Anatoly Lyadov just sat down at the piano
to play for his children.
Immaculately dressed
but completely relaxed,
he improvises a melody:
what poetry, what a gem!
"Say, Papa, can I sit on your lap?"

9 The Spinning Top
Georges Bizet (1838–1875)

The Spinning Top (La Toupie) is the second and shortest piece in *The Children's Games (Jeux d'enfants)*, Opus 22.

Wound as tight as can be, the spinning top makes a noise like thunder
as it dances about the whole room!
Bit by bit, it grows weary
and slows to a stop.
That won't do! Wind it up again
and boom, it starts off anew!
And again!

10 The Porcelain Shepherd and His Flock

Arthur Lourié (1892–1966)

Arthur Lourié was a Russian composer born in St. Petersburg. Although he studied with Alexander Glazunov, the most academic composer in the Russian capital, he went on to be one of the most avant-garde composers of his time. His cycle of children's pieces called *Piano Gosse* is not typical of his usual pianistic style but nonetheless reveals an exceptional personality.

On a bookshelf in a bedroom,
a flock of porcelain sheep and their shepherd
shine in the moonlight.
As the child falls asleep,
she sees them gently move and come to life.

11 Procession
Claude Debussy (1862–1918)

Procession (Cortège) is the second piece in Claude Debussy's *Short Suite (Petite Suite)*. Like *In a Boat (En bateau)*, it was inspired by Paul Verlaine's Fêtes Galantes.

Do you see the procession joyously passing by?
The tiny characters, fierce and heroic,
have lived a thousand adventures
and faced a thousand dangers.

12 The Sick Doll
13 The New Doll

Pyotr Ilyich Tchaikovsky (1840–1893)

Composed for his nephew Vladimir Davydov, Pyotr Ilyich Tchaikovsky's *The Children's Album*, Opus 39, contains music that is played by every Russian pianist. It is an essential collection in every music school in the land! Although often overplayed, these small pieces remain marvels of poetry, light, and tragedy.

*This much-loved doll
is always carried by Sophie
everywhere she goes.
She is worn out and quite sick.
This evening, Sophie watches over
her doll in the bedroom.
In the morning, behind the door, a new doll is waiting.
All her tears dry up.*

14 The Music Box, Opus 32
Anatoly Lyadov (1855–1914)

Blessed with many talents, Anatoly Lyadov was always a child at heart who endured life's vagaries in the hope of one day finding himself in a fairy tale!

Today, children, we are organizing
an exhibition of drawings,
a poetry reading, and my piano will imitate
a music box.
Life becomes a magical fairy tale!

15 Little Ugly Girl, Empress of the Pagodas
Maurice Ravel (1875–1937)

Composed between 1908 and 1910 for four-hand piano, *Mother Goose (Ma mère l'Oye)* is a suite based on the fairy tales of Charles Perrault, Jeanne-Marie Leprince de Beaumont, and Marie-Catherine d'Aulnoy. The latter wrote a tale entitled *The Green Streamer (Le Serpentin vert)*, which Maurice Ravel took as inspiration for the piece *Little Ugly Girl, Empress of the Pagodas (Laideronnette, impératrice des pagodes)*. Laideronnette, the hero of the fairy tale, is the victim of an evil curse cast by the cruel fairy, Magotine.

Laideronnette undressed and entered the bath.
Pagodas and pagodines immediately began to sing
and play musical instruments:
some had theorbos made of nutshells;
some had viols made of almond shells;
for the instruments had to be made to scale.

16 The Little White Donkey
Jacques Ibert (1890–1962)

Born in Paris, winner of the Grand Prix de Rome and later director of the Villa Médicis, Jacques Ibert composed many symphonic works, operas, ballets, and other genres. Curiously, however, his international reputation is based on one small piano piece: *The Little White Donkey (Le petit âne blanc)* from a 1922 collection entitled *Histoires*.

The little white donkey lightly strolls along, happy and without a care,
when, in the time it takes to dream,
he tastes freedom.
His braying becomes raucous and deep.
Upon waking, our little donkey resumes his stroll, even more lightly,
for he has touched the stars!

17 Egypt
Nikolai Tcherepnin (1873–1945)

Born the same year as Sergei Rachmaninoff, Nikolai Tcherepnin was one of several Russian composers considered to be disciples of an influential group known as The Five. *Fourteen Sketches on Pictures from the Russian Alphabet*, Opus 38, is inspired by pictures drawn by the great Russian artist Alexandre Benois. Entire generations have learned the Cyrillic alphabet from his drawings! Naturally, *Egypt* was composed for the letter "e."

The sky is vast,
a deep blue filled with stars
as far as the eye can see.
A single worrisome cloud
is a reminder of the nearby colossus
that watches over the sleeping dromedaries.

18 Music Box
Pierre Sancan (1916–2008)

An internationally renowned pianist and teacher, Pierre Sancan boasts an impressive list of famous students. Even though he was awarded the Prix de Rome, he is less well known for his own compositions. A small humorous treasure, *Music Box (Boîte à musique)* is one of his best-known piano pieces.

Ah, the poor old thing—
it's a music box!
It's seen better days,
needs some work,
is a bit out of tune—
but it plays.
The melody is quite pretty.
Where did it come from?
Who does it belong to?
Oh no, it stopped playing.

19 Lullaby
Gabriel Fauré (1845–1924)

Lullaby (Berceuse) is the first movement of *Dolly*, Opus 56, a suite of six pieces for four-hand piano written by Gabriel Fauré between 1894 and 1897. It was first performed in 1898 by Alfred Cortot and Édouard Risler.

Mama is here.
The room is enveloped in gentle tenderness.
A long day is over.
Sophie and Nicolas will soon be asleep.
All the day's emotions will then
disappear in the land of dreams.

20 The Magic Garden
Maurice Ravel (1875–1937)

The Magic Garden (Le jardin féerique) brings to a close *Mother Goose (Ma mère l'Oye)*, an imaginative suite composed by Maurice Ravel between 1908 and 1910.

So many musical works tell or illustrate fairy tales.
This ancient sarabande tells a different story:
the magic garden is itself a fairy tale,
and the music needs no words.

Musical selection, texts and performances
Ludmila Berlinskaïa and **Arthur Ancelle**
Illustrations **Élodie Nouhen**
Graphic Design **Frédérique Renoust** and **Stephan Lorti**
for **Haus Design** Translation **Hélène Roulston**
for **Service d'édition Guy Connolly**
Copy editor **Katherine Sehl**
Recording, mixing and mastering **Gaëtan Juge**

A unique code for the digital download of all recordings and a printable file of the text and illustrations is included with this book-CD. All recordings, under the title *Ma Boîte à musique*, are also available on several musical streaming platforms.

www.thesecretmountain.com
2022 The Secret Mountain (Folle Avoine Productions)
ISBN 978-2-89836-014-5

First published in France by Didier Jeunesse, Paris, 2021. All rights reserved. No part of this publication may be reproduced or transmitted in any form or by any means, electronic or mechanical, including photocopying, recording or any information storage and retrieval system, without permission in writing from the publisher. Printed in China.